The Patchworker

OXFORD

UNIVERSITY PRESS

The children were in the garden about to start a game – but they didn't have enough players. They needed one more person.

'Chip, go and get Anneena,' said Biff. 'Tell her we need her for the game.'

Chip ran into the house and found Anneena busy sewing a patchwork cover.

Chip stared at it and scratched his head. 'What's it supposed to be?' he asked.

'A cat, of course,' replied Anneena.

But all the pieces were muddled up. It didn't look like a cat at all!

'How ever did that happen?' said Anneena in surprise.

I don't know, but I wish she'd fix it, thought Floppy. How can you chase a cat that looks like that!

The key on Floppy's collar started to glow.

Suddenly Chip, Anneena, and Floppy were pulled into a spinning vortex of wonderful colours and dazzling lights. They were whirling round and round, faster and faster . . .

They landed in the middle of a patchwork desert where everything looked topsy-turvy. Soon they discovered a strange staircase that didn't seem to go anywhere. Anneena ran up the stairs to get a look at the view.

'It doesn't make any sense,' she called down. 'I've never seen a waterfall flowing upwards before.'

She ran back down to the others, but they couldn't get across the road because there were hundreds of fish swimming along it.

'Weird!' said Chip and Anneena.

How were they going to get across the road?

Look right, look left, look right again, thought Floppy. If there are no fish coming it's safe to cross, he chuckled to himself. At last all three of them walked safely to the other side.

The next thing they came to was a skyscraper – but it was upside down!

'She's put everything the wrong way up,' said a voice behind them.

'Or the wrong way round,' said another.

They looked round and saw some little pin people emerging from behind a rock.

'Who are you talking about?' asked Chip.

'The Patchworker, of course. Our ruler,' replied the pin people.

They looked up at the skyscraper. A little pin person was standing in the window of the very top floor.

'That's my husband up there,' said a pin person. 'He can't get down and I can't get up.'

Suddenly they heard the sound of marching footsteps coming their way.

'It's the Patchworker's guards,' cried the pin people. 'We've got to hide.'

One of them grabbed Anneena's hand and dragged her behind a rock. But Chip and Floppy were not so fast.

The leader of the guards, Major Darner, marched up to them.
'We arrest you on the orders of the Patchworker,' he said. 'You must come with us – immediately.'

Floppy whined anxiously, but they had no choice but to follow the guards away.

Chip and Floppy were marched to the Patchworker's castle and shown into a big room. There, sitting on a throne at one end of the room, was the Patchworker.

'You are not meant to be here,' she said. 'You are not part of the Pattern!'

'Part of the what?' asked Chip.

'The Pattern tells you where everything should go and how it all fits together,' replied the Patchworker.

This didn't make sense to Chip. He looked at the Patchworker with a puzzled expression. 'But it doesn't fit together,' he cried. 'Everything is in the wrong place.'

Floppy dropped to the floor and put his paws over his head. Major Darner gasped. 'You've done it now, son!' he said.

The Patchworker looked cross. She shook her finger at Chip and Floppy.

'Nobody ever questions the pattern!' she shouted.

Back in the desert, Anneena decided she must go in search of Chip and Floppy and rescue them.

'Tell the Patchworker that her people are very fed up!' cried the pin people. 'Tell her we want everything put in the right place.'

But Anneena didn't want to face the Patchworker on her own, so the pin people agreed to go along with her.

'But you have to be the leader,' they said.

From inside the castle the Patchworker could hear the pin people approaching.

'What's that noise?' she asked.

The Patchworker and Chip looked out of the window. All the pin people were shouting at once and they couldn't understand what they were trying to say.

'Who is that with them?' asked the Patchworker.

'It's my friend, Anneena!' replied Chip.

The Patchworker called to Major Darner, 'Bring Anneena to me!'

'Why are you here?' the Patchworker asked Anneena, as she entered the room.

Anneena gulped. She was *very* nervous.

'Er . . . I wanted to find my friends,' she said. 'And . . . er . . . your people are very unhappy. They can't get into their houses properly because they are upside-down. They can't use the roads because they are full of fish.'

'How dare you!' screamed the Patchworker. 'The people are neither here nor there. I follow the Pattern.'

And she reached into her trunk and pulled the Pattern out.

As they all looked at it, it was clear that everything on the Pattern was in the wrong place.

'Oh dear,' sighed the Patchworker. 'How did that happen?'

'You probably didn't check back with the picture to see if it matched,' said Anneena, showing her the picture on the box lid.

The Patchworker then sent Major Darner and his army to all the corners of Patchwork World to unpick all the mistakes and sew everything back together properly.

'Just a minute – don't forget this!' said Anneena, passing the box lid to Major Darner. 'Without the picture it won't make any sense.'

The pin people outside the castle cheered.

'Well done, Anneena,' they cried.

The Patchworker presented Anneena with a thimble from her trunk. This was the highest honour in the land, to thank her for all her help.

Anneena pointed to Floppy, who was curled up on the throne. 'The key's glowing,' she said. We're going, thought Floppy.

Back in the Robinsons' sitting room, Biff, Kipper, Wilma, and Wilf had come to find Chip and Anneena to see if they wanted to play the game.

'Sorry,' said Anneena, holding up the patchwork cover, 'but I've got to finish this for my mum's birthday.'

'And I'm helping,' said Chip.

'I have to check that the picture makes sense,' said Anneena.

'Well then, why don't we all help?' said Biff.

And they all sat down to help Anneena with her patchwork – which meant there was no seat left for Floppy.

Just my luck, he thought.

OXFORD
UNIVERSITY PRESS

Great Clarendon Street, Oxford OX2 6DP

Oxford University Press is a department of the University of Oxford.
It furthers the University's objective of excellence in research, scholarship,
and education by publishing worldwide in

Oxford New York

Athens Auckland Bankok Bogotá Buenos Aires
Cape Town Chennai Dar es Salaam Delhi Florence Hong Kong Istanbul
Kolkata Karachi Kuala Lumpur Madrid Melbourne Mexico City Mumbai
Nairobi Paris São Paulo Singapore Taipei Tokyo Toronto Warsaw

with associated companies in Berlin Ibadan

Oxford is a registered trade mark of Oxford University Press in the UK and in certain other countries

British Library Cataloguing in Publication Data available
ISBN 0-19-272434-7
3 5 7 9 10 8 6 4 2